Hours *of* Wealth

Hours *of* Wealth

STORIES

Joshua *W.* James

Teksteditions
Toronto

Editor: Beverley Daurio
Associate editor: Richard Truhlar
Cover design: Beverley Daurio with Joshua W. James
Page design and composition: Beverley Daurio

First Edition

1 2 3 4 5   2016 2015 2014 2013 2012

James, Joshua W.
     Hours of wealth / Joshua W. James.

Short stories.
Issued also in an electronic format.
ISBN 978-1-927367-21-6 (bound).--ISBN 978-1-927367-19-3 (pbk.)

     I. Title.

PS8619.A633H68 2012   C813'.6   C2012-906932-9

Softcover: 978-1-927367-19-3
Electronic: 978-1-927367-20-9
Hardcover: 978-1-927367-21-6

Teksteditions
www.teksteditions.com

Contents

This was always for you.

"Pooh began to feel a little more comfortable, because when you are a Bear of Very Little Brain, and you Think of Things, you find sometimes that a Thing which seemed very Thingish inside you is quite different when it gets out into the open and has other people looking at it."

—A.A. Milne: *The House at Pooh Corner*

Evander

▼

One Tuesday, Evander started drawing triangles on the floor. It happened quite suddenly, and just before breakfast. He was depressed because the C.N. Tower had spent the better part of a week with its upper third stuck in the clouds. No one had asked him to elaborate. The only one who seemed to understand Evander was Evander, and that day he stopped talking altogether.

He was in the middle of making breakfast — toast had just popped, an unread newspaper spread out on the table beside his orange juice — and he looked at the floor, tiled white and speckled with bits of dried cat food in one corner. He took the pencil that he had sharpened specially for his crossword puzzle and sat on the floor, oblivious to his fellow breakfasters, and began to scribble triangles into the tiles, one after the other.

Those in his company shrugged and assumed he had come up with something none of them would understand anyway, so why bother spoiling a good meal? When his roommates arrived home that night and more than half the walls in the apartment were covered with triangles, they thought there might be a serious problem.

He *does* seem pretty crazy. Poor Evander. I mean, he rocks and hums and stares, when he's not drawing his triangles, that is. One of his roommates still visits him, the other having been frightened that the autism, or whatever the know-it-alls want to call it, might be contagious.

She tries to talk to him, as everyone does, but there he sits.

Can you see him? Swaying, his eyes kind of dazed, deep in thought, so you can almost see the triangles buzzing behind his eyes if you look hard enough. Give him a pen or crayon and out come the triangles. Over and over. Each one connected to the next. Like puzzle pieces. If they take away the crayons and the pens, he tries to scratch his shapes into the floor with his fingernails. They give him building blocks to play with, and are pleased when he uses them. Eureka! A breakthrough! The unfathomable Evander has finally broken his trance! But, alas, the blocks he lines up start to form triangles. One of the nurses in his ward quit, exclaiming that if she ever sees another triangle she'll hit someone.

He isn't too difficult with eating his meals, even if sometimes his Cheerios are stacked up in the shape of triangles, and he doesn't fuss about bathing or letting the nurses help him dress or go to the bathroom. He is a pleasant fellow, if one doesn't mind another human being who will not communicate with them, will not sympathize or criticize or show emotion, or talk about baseball or video games. Actually, trying to relate to Evander is like trying to rhyme with "orange." Porridge, forage, no...not quite. You have to tolerate Evander on another level. You can't be too picky. You must be passive, and not mind being ignored. And, at the very least, you have to accept his triangles. As you can imagine, many of the employees of the Dawnview Home for the befuddled draw straws to decide who spends time with him.

Eventually, in a room, left to his own devices, Evander's pattern of triangles grows to monstrously complex proportions. It is strange how, up close, it is a dizzying jumble of triangles, but pull back a bit and, lo!, it seems to form a string here, and a sphere there. Knots of shapes formed by shapes formed by triangles. Turn your head a bit, and…most of the people shake their heads and assume that the triangles are driving them all mad too! Perhaps it *is* contagious, for we all start to see shapes in his scrawlings, like cloud gazers under a speckled sky.

If left long enough, something strange happens to Evander. He becomes agitated, tracing over pre-existing triangles and fidgeting. Why does this happen? One of the attendants jokingly says that he is simply an *autist* suffering from a block!

His dilemma is revealed only by an outsider, a visiting student, who is writing a thesis on autism, named Dolores. Evander has been removed from his room so that the janitor can clean off the floor and walls. He is given a pencil and some paper and told to behave for Dolores. No one really knows if he listens to this, but feels it proper to say so anyway, perhaps so that they won't feel responsible if he suddenly snaps and does something really nutty.

—Isn't it kind of mean to destroy all that work he's done? asks the young student as she looks over the intricate webbing of interconnected triangles.

—Oh, it's okay, says the attendant. —He'll just fill it all up again. We've timed him. It takes twelve hours, give or take, to fill the entire room. Except for the clear patch he leaves himself on the floor to sleep in. We figure, give him a box of pencils just after lunch and he'll be asleep by midnight. We spend the morning cleaning his room, and start him again after lunch.

—Why does he get so frustrated?

—Who knows? Besides him, I mean. He stopped talking three years ago last week, I think. Evander keeps his own secrets.

Dolores looks over the room. —There isn't really any furniture.

—He doesn't like furniture. You can't really draw on a bedspread. Or a cushion. He puts them out in the hall.

She runs her hand over the walls, and then crouches on the floor.

—Look how the drawing gets smaller and smaller.

—Yeah, he gets pretty intricate. If you look at some of the larger triangles that frame the smaller patches, you'll notice that they are mathematically perfect. Straight, perfect lines. Drawn without the aid of rulers or any other straight edge. It is humanly impossible to do that. But there they are.

—There was an autistic child in Ottawa who could draw a perfect circle with a sweep of her hand. And another here in Toronto, an old woman who could draw architecture and buildings and other non-living objects with stunning intricacy, yet she could not draw faces or anything organic. But this...this is impressive. Look how tiny...

She stops. Looks closer, scrunches up her face, and looks closer still.

—Oh, oh. Not you too, says the attendant, worried that she has gone nuts right in front of him.

—He can't go any smaller, says Dolores.

—I'm sorry, could you say that again?

—He cannot draw any smaller. Look at these dots and scribbles here. They aren't triangles. They are failed attempts. It is impossible for him to draw them any smaller than this one here...

—I can barely even see that one.

—And so he has to stop?

They rush to where Evander is waiting for them, in an adjacent room, with pencil and paper in hand, and Dolores kneels beside him. In just under an hour, the picture on the sheet is already mind-bogglingly complex. She looks at it a moment, then beckons the attendant.

—May I have another sheet of paper.

—Don't you start, too, he says, handing her the sheet.

She looks at Evander and then back at the attendant.

—Go ahead. He never gets angry. He'll just start over like nothing happened.

Dolores gently takes the picture away from Evander and places the blank sheet in front of him. He pauses a moment, looking at it, cocks his head, and begins again without a fret. She pores over the picture, and then dashes from the room.

—Dolores, is there something you need to tell us? puffs the attendant, darting after her.

—Yeah, you have a miracle in your care.

—A who?

—A damned miracle!

—Excuse me, miss, but I don't personally believe that there is anything miraculous about sketching thousands of triangles.

—You don't understand yet, that's why.

—What are you doing?

Dolores studies the sheet, walking around the graffitied room. From sheet to wall to sheet to floor she chases something elusive to the attendant.

—There! she exclaims after a time.

—Where?

She kneels down in the corner, near the blank spot where, presumably, he sleeps, all curled up. Near the section that shapes his head, she puts down the sheet and the attendant is shocked to see the lines match up perfectly.

—My God, he breathes.

—It fits. Evander is drawing exactly the same thing, over and over. I mean exactly. Each time he starts again, the same size. Same angles. Same patterns, in the same order. It isn't random. I'm afraid, sir, that Evander isn't necessarily mad. He knows exactly what he's doing.

It is unthinkable. But there it is, plain as day. Identical. Perhaps he *is* a miracle.

Who, or what, is Evander anyway? I mean, before his fixations. One could say that the universe was once a singularity, a point of zero dimensions, which had infinite mass. This point, invisible, but alive with all time, history, creation, and everything in between, existed as a heartbeat between universes, a bridge. Before that, it was an entirely different universe than the one we hurtle through. Evander is no exception. Dolores wants to identify his motives. His point of origin.

—You are born autistic. You die autistic. There isn't anything modern science can tell you as far as cause and effect go, and nothing medicine can do to stop it. It is an incurable defect of the brain, much like mental retardation, that plagues a person for life. One cannot simply sit down on the floor one day and become autistic, I don't care what may have happened to him.

Dolores hates the professor's tone. She clears her throat and tries to find a serious, non-threatening cadence for her own response.

—You're absolutely correct. I'm not denying that, although I might add it hasn't actually been proven, either.

He frowns at her.

—I just want to point out that with no real empirical evidence to suggest that this absolutely can't happen, I'm willing to follow through investigating even the most remote chance that...

—That what? One could catch autism as if it were a virus?

—Well, no. But Evander is a very special case. His behaviour, his symptoms, his fixation, all of it suggests some form of autism. Yet, you say, how could that be? As we know, he was born quite normal, by any standards. And there is no reason to assume something traumatic happened to him the morning he lapsed into his...state.

—To be honest with you, Miss Mckinnen, I don't believe Evander Clark is autistic. He is obsessive-compulsive. He has functional disorders. He is most certainly anti-social. I am unwilling to accept he merely shut down one morning like a transmitter.

—But he is shut down. He exhibits all the signs of what we call autism. He is unable to communicate. He cannot decipher motives, or tell the difference between feigned emotions and genuine ones. He doesn't appear to have any higher cognitive reasoning available to him. But he did at one point. He was normal.

—How do you know he isn't putting on a show?

—Well, you can tell by looking at him...

—Oh, come now. You can do better than that, the professor says.

—When I sit next to him, I feel like I am in a room by myself. When he looks at you, it is with the same response he might give a wall, or a door, as though people to him are simply objects. The only time he looks at you is when you take away his pencils or paper.

—Tell me about these triangles.

—They are actually the best evidence I have to present for the existence of his disability. In fact, they seem to be the core.

—Say again?

—Is it possible for someone to draw a perfect circle, I mean mathematically perfect, with a single, freehanded stroke without an aide of any fashion?

—Of course not.

—But it has been documented that an autistic child living in Ottawa can do it. Autism takes away something the rest of us have. I don't know, maybe it's empathy, and higher cognitive reasoning, and self-awareness, maybe a lot of things. But it appears to give as well. Like acute sensitivity to sound in the blind. Some autistic people learn to speak fluidly before the age of five. Others are mathematical geniuses, but will not know how to respond if you ask them how they feel.

—So how do the triangles prove that Evander isn't just putting us all on?

—The whole thing is a diagram of some sort. If left with the means to work for an extended length of time, and given enough space to grow, the triangles become structured and form distinct patterns. It is performed with a pre-existing knowledge of itself as a whole, and he is repeating it.

—The triangles, I know...

—No, the whole thing. He does it identically each time, not necessarily starting in the same place, either. Matching areas from two separate occasions can be aligned without the slightest discrepancy or break in the lines. This image...whatever it is, is complete, perfectly intact, in his head. Now, I could just be shooting at the moon here, but I suspect that it occupies the space where all his normal brain activity used to occur. He has one thing on his mind, but that one thing has taken up so much space that everything else has been displaced.

—How big do you expect this...image is?

—I don't know. But I suppose you could ask how much space is in the mind and find that it fits, one way or another. The only way to know is to let him draw it out.

—You'll fill up an awful lot of paper, the professor says.

—That is why we've given him a computer.

The professor sighs, visibly intrigued.

—You really feel you are on to something here, don't you.

—Evander is the one on to something. I am just jotting down what I see.

Dolores realizes upon hearing her own voice how similar this is to Evander himself. Isn't he just jotting down whatever it is he sees in his head?

—Okay, Dolores. You have your extension. Bring me a good one.

When word about something like this gets around, people begin to whisper, and squint their eyes around corners or half-opened doorways. What is the big secret? Evander Clark, the looney up on five, is drawing something that everyone, whether they like it or not, is interested in. I mean, if you could just see it for yourself, you too would feel it. You might turn to your co-observers and huff and say that it really wasn't such a big deal. Impressive, but a sham. Secretly, you might wonder about it. One can't help it. I saw it myself. It is nothing short of a miracle.

It really doesn't take long to teach the software interface to Evander, despite his unresponsive nature. A computer teacher, borrowed by Dolores from the university, sits with him and makes examples of how to sketch lines and drag circles with the mouse. As soon as he is shown the option that draws triangles using this click and drag technique, he subtly sweeps the teacher's hand aside and delves into it. Within hours his network of triangles is taking shape on the glowing screen. The way the glow mirrors his blank eyes is haunting.

The program is a wonder in itself, really. Some of the attendants will pore over it in the wee hours of the night, drawing stick-men and generic sunsets. You can flip your drawings, and animate them, and rotate them in three-dimensional space, and shine light on them at any point you wish, and add texture. Anything. You can make it become real. No one has really expected to see Evander's triangles become multi-dimensional, though, and it is chilling when they do. Retrospectively, Dolores wonders if flatness could have contributed to his frustration. Whatever the case, he can zoom in to infinitely small scales and draw the tiniest triangles ever.

Dolores is examining the image, Evander being asleep in his room. Who would have ever thought it could become this? She rotates it, tingles running through her. It looks like some kind of machine imagined by Einstein or Carl Sagan or someone. She wonders what it will be when it is complete, if it is ever complete? Maybe not. Maybe it is like an unending number? The zeros just continue on forever. What then? Well, she will see when that happens. She feels helpless. She feels like adding a triangle herself, but hasn't got a clue where to add one. Where do you start? How does Evander know which one to draw next, and where? She sneaks a little one in anyway, hooked onto a triangle twice its size.

There, she thinks.

As sure as she is sitting here watching him, Evander spins the image, surveying its convoluted geometry, and quickly finds the alien triangle she drew. She is in awe. He ponders it a moment, looking at it with confusion on his face, and then he deletes the shape. It simply doesn't belong, she imagines him saying. Well, as tough as it is to imagine him saying anything.

The attendant beckons her from the room.

—I guess that just proves even more that this thing is completely intact in his head, he says.

—But where. Where is it kept?

Dolores shakes her head.

—When I was younger we lived on the Danforth, he says. —There was a church, Holy Name it was called, that was just around the corner. It was where I was baptised and confirmed and such, you know. Anyway, I'm not an incredibly religious man, but I still consider that church a defining structure in my life. It was this magnificent building that I always felt special visiting. I must have gone through its doors a thousand times, but I can't remember how many windows it had, or how many pews or confessionals. I try and visualize its outer face in my mind, and I get an incomplete impression, a feeling. If I went back, I would stand before it and nod at every corner and window, but that sort of thing leaves my mind quickly. How is it that that man in there stores something of such size in his brain? Where does it go?

—My question is where it came from. How it got there, Dolores says.

—Some of the other attendants talk about it. Sometimes with me, sometimes in lowered voices.

—What do they think?

—Aliens? Or maybe a message from God. Or maybe the government put it there? He says this almost in a whisper.

—In Canada? Or do you mean that the Americans are implanting blueprints in Canadian heads? Dolores says, smiling to herself.

The attendant blinks.

—Never mind.

—Well, I guess I just wanted to share my bewilderment with someone. With you, he says.

—To be honest with you, I can't even begin to imagine what it means. But to Evander, it's something, and that's enough for me.

▶ ▼ ▼ ▲

With a jolt she springs out of bed and switches off her
alarm. Dolores no longer enjoys breakfast as a leisurely
event; she scarfs it up from where it lies on her lap as the subway hurtles toward the East End of the city. Her hair is half-
brushed, her clothes creased. She has developed pouches under
her eyes and calluses between her writing fingers. I've seen her
on several occasions of late, standing amidst the morning subway rush, struggling to keep her balance as the car jostles back
and forth. She is tired and distracted. She is like a child who
has to spend time away from her new toy. If I, or any other
soul on this early morning train, were to ask her what is
wrong, I'm afraid the only thing that would occur to her
would involve a young man and his triangles. I've got a lot on
my mind, she would say. Evander is on her mind, and I know
that is a lot. I think about him, too.

Dolores squints and peers at everything. Buildings, cars,
faces…all require her strict attention. She studies angles and
features and shapes. Perhaps she is waiting for it to be revealed
to her that everything is made up of millions of tiny triangles,
forming into their respective larger shapes. She is sure that the
answer, one way or the other, will become clear if she just
looks close enough.

She comes to the building. The knob is round. The door
is rectangular. The marble tiles beneath her feet in the lobby,
square, are decorated with flowers…all ovals and fractal stems.
At the end of the lobby, an attendant stands statue-still. He
looks at her. His eyes are like almonds.

—Today, he says, —at about lunchtime, Evander stopped.
She looks at the Asian man with a fold in her brow.

—Stopped?

—Drawing triangles.

In the pulse between seconds that bridges the space between her befuddlement and her panic, it is noted by her brain that the lights, diamond, are much too bright in here. Then she runs for the elevator. Sliding doors…floor buttons…a bell dinging…lengthy, carpeted hallway…an empty chair in front of a deserted computer terminal. The screen is blank. She looks around, scanning the room for signs of Evander, of which there are none. She sits in the seat and switches the computer on. It whirs and blinks to life, little lights flashing at the base of the monitor. When the system is booted up, she opens the drawing program that they taught Evander to use. The file containing her miracle, simply called "evander," is not there. There are, in fact, no files in the program. All traces of his work are gone. A strange feeling sweeps over her.

—He finished, comes a voice.

Turning, she sees a nurse standing in the doorway.

—Where is it?

—Gone.

Dolores feels flushed. She feels an ache in her belly. She realizes that her life had been on hold pending Evander's revelation.

—What do you mean it's gone? It can't be gone, she laughs in reassurance of herself. There must be a back-up copy. The file must be recoverable.

—I'm sorry, Dolores. He wiped it all from the system.

—He doesn't know how to wipe everything from the system. Does he?

—I think everything will be easier if you just come and see him.

Dolores curses and follows the nurse. They board the elevator and take it down to the first floor cafeteria. Within, Dolores can see Evander, sitting and eating a bagel. He is talking to someone.

—Is he...

—He just stood up, muttered something, and then asked for a bagel. It was too late when we realized that he'd wiped the file.

—What word?

—Sorry?

—You said he uttered a word. What was it?

—I didn't catch it, to be honest. Is it important?

Dolores leaves the company of the nurse and pushes her way into the cafeteria. Evander sees her, but he shows no sign of recognizing her. All those days she spent with him. All those hours she sat in the room with him...it is as if they never happened.

—Evander...she begins.

—Well, he says. —You must be the tenth person claiming to know me today. I must admit, you all have the advantage. Apparently, my reputation precedes me.

—Do you remember nothing?

He chews on his bagel, speaking in between mouthfuls.

—Oh. This and that.

Dolores is aghast. She barely knows what to say.

—Well...how do you feel?

—Fine. It's a nice day. This is a great bagel. I feel refreshed, I think.

She can't hold back. It just blurts out.

—What about your triangles?

He looks at her emotionlessly.

—What about them?

—What do they mean? What is it all about?

He shrugs, and the person he is talking to, presumably

his prior roommate, draws his attention. Disappointed, she turns around, spotting an attendant nearby.

—I suppose you weren't there when he finished, were you?

—As a matter of fact, I was.

—And did you hear what he said?

—I believe it was simply, *Never mind.*

She shakes her head.

—Have you never changed your mind before? he asks.

Dolores frowns, casts her gaze to the door, and says simply, —Excuse me, I've got a deadline.

The next morning, Evander is released from Dawnview. He smiles and shakes hands with a few attendants and patients, then quietly slips out into the morning sun. A few of us stand by the staff room window on the third floor and watch him walk to the end of the tree-lined walkway. He stops and squints, shading his eyes against the sun, hesitating, as though he cannot decide which way he should go, then disappears behind the polished stone of the walled garden.

Billy, Beleaguered

In class today we're dissecting a pale frog. Later, in bed with Noreen on her parent's unreasonably thick duvet, I'm thinking that her winter-pallid legs are familiar somehow. The way they are splayed, bowed at the knees, unmoving, sinking into the mauve floral-print quicksand we're lying on, and I'm stricken by the sharp instinct to escape.

I retreat to the washroom and use a towel to clean myself. I splash water on my face. There are pills in her medicine cabinet. I don't know what they are, but they are pretty and blue and I take three of them. When I return I can't decide if the room smells like sex or formaldehyde. Only a soft sun filters through the thick curtains, and in the half-light Noreen looks pale grey, still akimbo on the bed. If she hadn't reached up and lit a cigarette, I'd have thought her dead. For a moment the yellow leaf of flame shines on her face, and it leaves behind a cherry glow. She sucks the filter. The cherry flares, then dims. That burnt tobacco smell passes my nose and I wrinkle it.

—You gonna stand there all day? she says. I can't see her features in the shadowy room, but I can feel her turn and look at me. I can just make out the pasty slope of one leg as it dangles off the edge of the bed, the tip of her big toe brushing the rug.

—Absolutely not, I say, crouching and patting the carpet, finding my briefs. I yank them up and then sit on the edge of the bed near her. The duvet is cool against the underside of my legs. I feel her hand on my back.

—So I'm curious, she says. —Was that it, or what? What happens next?

—Well, next I have to make my way home.

She clucks her teeth. —I don't just mean today. I mean in general.

Was that a hint of resentment creeping into her voice?

—I mean, was this just a one-time thing, or do we see each other again, or what?

I glance at her in the gloom.

—I'm indifferent, she adds.

She seems to be genuine, harbouring no expectation. But, for a reason I can't explain, I feel a pang of etiquette. I'm almost compelled to make this tryst more than it is, just to lubricate my exit from her life. I don't wish her any grief, but it just sort of comes out, much the way one says "*Bless you*" when someone sneezes. Inside the grey folds of my mind there resides a line of code, a ground rule, that says *sex is never just sex*. Nothing good is free, and therefore sex must be paid for. Promises are the fee. A currency of kisses and commitment. I'm just a satisfied customer, and it's time to pay the proverbial whore.

I think she says —I leave it up to you to decide what this is really about. But outside a car horn blares and garbles her words.

—Of course we can see each other again, I say. —Maybe even tomorrow.

She is quiet for a moment. I sense that she's interpreting my words. Deciding if what I really mean is "so long, and thanks for the fish." She comes to some quiet conclusion, sucks the end of her cigarette in a long draw, the heater's glow shimmering faintly in her brown eyes. I get the impression that she is taciturn; emotionally guarded. She has been hurt in the past, no doubt, and hesitates before getting involved. Old wounds ache when rain is approaching. An emotional limb is still aware of itself long after it has been amputated. I bet she can feel it itching sometimes late at night when she is alone.

This all makes my guilt worse.

—I don't want to leave, I say. I'll probably think of you all night.

—Really? she says too anxiously. A crack appears in her façade of indifference, and through it I glimpse certain hopefulness, like blood in shark waters.

—Well yeah, I say, nudging her nude leg beside me. —I'm not letting you get away that easy.

She says nothing. In the darkness, I can feel her smile. She breathes out a plume of smoke.

—I can already see that you're going to be very addictive, I add. Just for good measure.

Just to up the ante.

And now I can leave, guilt-free, to join the parade of the faithless out on the twilit streets. We are legion.

The ersatz face of Tesla gleams at me, leans in, skin half-lit by the candle between us. I'd run screaming from it if I didn't want to fuck it. That face, full as the moon, and just as waning. She tells me about her day, about something that happened by the photocopy machine, but I can't be bothered listening to her. I find I can ignore someone if I freeze my face in a certain accommodating expression. They go on with their one-sided conversation, unaffronted, and I'm free to think about whatever. But her voice is infirm, as though she is hiding an incredible vulnerability that reveals itself vocally, and it often distracts me from pretending she doesn't exist. Dinner was necessary, I think, in getting Tesla to trust me enough to come home with me. But all this aftertalk, it's moot. At this point we're just prolonging the inevitable. I am a lion and the calf is already down. I'm just pacing beside it, delaying gratification.

There is no purer moment, no taste more bitter, than the instant the final grain of pleasure falls through the centre of the hourglass. When the orgasm is over. When the event you'd been waiting for is past, and you realize it had been what you were holding your breath for. When anticipation becomes memory. When something is in the past, it possesses the power to consume you, like a predator that has been stalking you since the moment you were born, lulling you with memories so that you lie back, complaisant, sedated by nostalgia, presenting an easy target. You can think of nothing else when you are stuck there, derailed, a wreckage of longing and perhaps regret, thrown to the side of the road.

This is what I'm thinking about as I poke my crab linguini. Seafood before sex invites uncomfortable comparisons. By the time my parfait comes, I'm layered with a sweaty pall of regret.

Ever order a meal and realize when it comes that it isn't what you really wanted?

Before I can help myself, I start giggling. She stops in mid-sentence, and blinks at me.

—What's funny? she says, and she's so sincere that I laugh even louder.

The world ends not with a bang, but with a guffaw, and I know I'm running perilously close to losing this one. Before she can take offense to my scene, I salvage the situation as best I can.

—Just how things turn out, you know?

Tesla nods her head in a way that tells me she has no clue what the fuck I'm talking about, but wants to agree with me anyway.

—I mean, we're here now. If you had told me last week, or even yesterday, that I'd be sitting in a restaurant with the most beautiful woman in Toronto, I'd have thought you mad.

She smiles, her face still a little blank. She has that unfocused look in her eyes, like a tranquilized goat. She manages to blush, however. She murmurs an appreciation for my compliment. She even laughs a little.

Ten minutes later I'm paying the bill with my parents' credit card. It is nearly a quarter past seven. Before eight o'clock I'm at her house with my hand up her blouse. She seems to like her tits touched, though personally I couldn't care less about them. When I remove her dress she's wearing a pink g-string. It's amusing when you find this, because it means she was expecting someone to look there. Amusing because it is contrary to the air of unaffected naivety she'd been giving off all evening. G-strings certainly aren't worn for comfort's sake. No, this spaghetti-strap lingerie was worn for the express purpose that she supposed I would be here, doing what I'm doing. I don't know whether to be flattered or aghast at her assumption. Of course, I'm probably just hopelessly self-indulgent here, taking for granted that she knows, *has known* all along what I'm really about.

I hook two fingers under her silky panties and yank them off. I'm sure she wanted me to comment on them or something. I have no use for eccentric lingerie. To me it's all garnish on the plate.

Funny how you want something only up till the moment it is certain to be yours.

I'm looking down at her ridiculous expressions. She's flushed, her eyes pinched together. Why people do that I don't know. Either it's to fling yourself into some kind of fantasy, to enhance copulation, or else it's because you can't stand to look at the person you are fucking. Her mouth is open, closed, open, closed. Making oh's, like a goldfish. And she's saying stuff too, but it's distracting me so I block it out by groaning loud. I hate making noise during sex, but it's worse when they do it. One thing she says does get through, though. A name. She says —Simon… and sort of purrs after. My name isn't Simon, but it only bothers me for a moment because I'm too busy trying to keep my balance. My knee keeps slipping off the edge of the bed. There is an instant of panic when I notice she has the exact same bedspread as Noreen, that mauve floral-print duvet. Wait, I think… is this Noreen? No… Noreen was way skinnier. This must be Deborah. By face I can't tell, but it's remarkable how similar their duvets are.

She must sense my distraction, because her eyes are open, and she reaches up and touches my face. She smiles.

—What's wrong? she says.

—Nothing, I say and the way her eye catches the light from a blue halogen lamp clipped to the headboard reminds me of this other time I was with a girl called Morrigan. She was fucked up, Morrigan was. I ran into her at the mall and asked her for a cigarette. On the basis of that very innocent first impression, I found myself bending her over a park bench later that night. Just a few minutes before the bench situation, she'd said to me, —How do you wanna do it?

I mean, I'm not a lewd person. This is the sort of thing I'm not used to talking about openly. It's also dangerous. Picture a kid in a toy store, and mommy says —So… what do you want?

Given the circumstances, I think I chose rather generically. And so, the park bench. Silver moon bright enough to cast shadows. Up the length of her body, past the pom-pom of her wool hat, I can see a mist of breath wisp out of her mouth. My hands shiver as I hook my thumbs under her pantline and drag them down to her knees. Her white panties are luminous by moonlight, but I'm drawn to the darkness between her thighs. Her pudenda are but a shadowy mound. A hot refuge in the frigid air. I stuff myself into the shadow, and she sighs. A wreath of breath steams up around her head as I give a blur of furious thrusts. As cold as it is, I manage a feeble semi-orgasm. I withdraw, careful not to soil my clothes, and when I'm out of her there is a flapping sound. Something black-winged flutters out and up into the night sky, disturbing the branches of a tree that hangs over us. It unseats the last remaining leaf gripped in the clawed branches. The leaf spirals down. My face is upturned, watching the black bird (if indeed that's what it is) and the leaf gently hits my forehead. With that soft touch, there is a tremendous booming eruption deep within me, like the echo of heavy artillery fired in the dead of night. Morrigan is pulling up her pants and saying something.

Deborah is pulling up her pants and she says —You seem distant.

I'm not that far away, actually. Just a few years ago, on the other side of town. From the corner of the room, there is a fluttering sound… wind blowing the curtains.

She says —I can feel you dripping inside me.

Today, in class, I thought I'd seen the frog move. Pale and rubbery and split wide open. I'd been poking its insides with my pen and I swore, just for a moment, I saw it move. A slight twitch of leg. But it was fleeting, and as hard as I stared I did not see it move again. And there's only so long you can stare bug-eyed at a dead frog before the people around you start backing away. Perhaps I'd imagined it.

—I think we should go to Naples this year, says Deborah, and I can't remember if I'm married to her. No, we're still in high school, so we can't be married. Who is she?

—Well? She says, sitting on the edge of the bed, staring up at me like a child.

—Hi, I say. Sorry, I zoned out for a moment there.

—No kidding. Do you want to go with me to Staples? I need to get some printer paper.

Just for a moment, I thought maybe it was something more. Just for a flash of a second, I thought I might have seen it move. Just a spark of life.

—You better get dressed, she says, pointing at my cock, which sticks out in front of me like a flaccid balloon, still dribbling spit from one end.

She kisses me.

—Hmm... your breath tastes like coffee, cigarettes, and pussy, she says. There's some Listerine in the washroom.

The washroom is too bright, and I think it works much the same way as an x-ray. Under its glare, I can see right through myself. Bones, veins, secrets, everything.

Deborah is knocking at the door.

—Well, are you coming or not? she says.

And I'm thinking what the fuck happened to the condom? Did she have it? Did I throw it out already?

—Where? I ask, tearing my eyes away from the reflection of the man in the mirror and snooping through the medicine cabinet. There are these blue pills in there. What the fuck are these anyway? I've seen them in other girl's washrooms too. I pop a few just so I don't feel left out.

—Naples. My father owns… blah blah blah… And then she trails off.

—Deb? I call, but I choke on Listerine.

Then there is a deep voice from downstairs. And she's at the door again.

—I said, hurry, my dad's home!

I cough up some Listerine. The mirror is like an MRI… I can see my inner child.

—*Are you hurrying?*

Outside, she gives me her keys and says —You drive. I hate the truck.

The interior of the pick-up is silent and still, waiting for someone to give it the spark of life. Sort of like Deborah.

—Have you ever been to Naples? I ask.

—What? she says. She looks at me, staring full blast as though trying to figure out if I'm insulting her.

—Naples.

—Where is that?

She rifles through her purse, pulling out cigarettes and a lighter.

—Isn't it in… I sort of stop in mid-sentence, bored by my own train of thought. —Would you ever suck my dick while driving?

—Just shut up and drive, she says, lighting her cigarette.

When you have this sort of open-concept relationship with someone, you have lots of space to let your demons out and still have room to move. Mom says Deborah is spouse-material. A real keeper. Or wait… that's Vivian.

Deborah is talking. About food, I think.

—I feel like eating out tonight, I say. Wanna come?

Deborah flicks an ash out the window and mumbles in response.

At least, I think her name is Deborah. Suddenly I'm not sure. You can put it softly, casually, even humorously, but no matter how you say it, asking a girl you've just fucked to remind you what her name is never sounds good. I don't bother. So many problems are solved by asking yourself, *Do I really care?*

I wait in the car while she goes into the store. When she's out of sight, I drive away, leaving her there. There is a fluttering sound behind me. In the rearview mirror, I think I can see something flapping.

—Hellloooooo…?

I open my eyes.

Dimly lit in a silent and unfamiliar room, Vivian is staring at me with eyes like globes.

—Billy, are you okay? she says. You just drifted away there. What's wrong with you lately?

—I'm fine. Just… tired.

—I thought you really wanted to come to Italy. Come on, sunshine and Naples! She shakes me playfully. Ever since we got here, you've felt like you were somewhere else.

She looks at me, her expression soft and concerned.

—Everything is fine. I… love you?

I don't know why the last two words emerge as a question, but she doesn't react. I kiss her, and we walk along the busy street.

A dark bird flies across the sky.

I look up at the moment the tremors begin. The ground buckles, and my knees wobble. I nearly lose balance, and Vivian looks at me with a flash of fear. The ground shakes horribly, and a roar rises so swiftly that I have no time to shield my ears. Deafened by the murmur of the earth, we are narrowly missed as a storefront collapses along the street, as though it had merely been a prop. I see Vivian's eyes grow wide, and I follow her gaze. The sky is becoming black.

She's saying —No no no…

And I grab her hand.

As we run for higher ground, the streets are chaos. A wave of panic storms through the market, and here we are, running against the tide. Ahead I see a large tower, probably a place of worship, tumble and fall into the street, spewing dust and rubble everywhere, clouding the air. The ground heaves, and I fight to stay on my feet. Vivian, her nails digging into the flesh of my palm, screams behind me. In the distance, I can see the cracking Greco-Roman façade of the Villa Medici, where we were staying. One entire side of it collapses.

—Billy! she calls, but I am running.

The sky is nearly black when at last we reach the hill of Posillipo. Mud and ash hit my face as I climb, and Vivian drops to her knees, weeping.

—Come on! I yell, but she is not moving.

So I leave her. Once I look back as I scramble up the shuddering hillside, pelted incessantly by falling debris. I can barely make out her form in the growing darkness. She's on hands and knees, patting the ground around her as though she is desperately searching for some lost thing. For a moment I consider running back to her; she must be so afraid. But from behind me there comes such a tremendous thunder, as though the earth itself is rent open and its bowels are howling into the blackening sky. I press on, and at last reach the summit.

Before me, the hill drops and I can see the bay of Naples, and across the water Mount Vesuvius is blown wide open. From its summit a horrible tower of black rises and scrapes across the sky, churning with rock and ash. Weak sunlight filters through, but the slopes of the angry mountain are lit red with streaks of fire. Lava spits from the crown and broils in the plume, and down on the bay I can see molten rain descending on the harbours. Even the water is burning in places, and I realize there are ships down there, nothing more than sailing infernos now. My head swims in delirium, so thick with ash is the air I breathe. Wave after wave of ground shock cracks the hillside, and a tree that had been standing close to my vantage point is no longer there. I'm slipping, my feet in a bog of mud that flows down the hill towards a residential area that swirls with flame. As I ride the river of sliding earth I pass a dog chasing its own burning tail.

—I think I should go, says Shelly. She is pulling up one stocking.

—Where? I ask, blinking. What the hell time is it?

—Home.

—Look, I'm sorry, I say. This has never happened to me before.

She looks at me for a moment, then says, —If someone you were sucking off fell asleep, you'd leave too.

—I told you, I wasn't asleep. My eyes were closed in … ecstasy.

—Billy. She says my name as though it is vulgar.

—Aw, give me a little credit, will you? I mean, honestly, who falls asleep during sex?

—It wasn't sex, it was foreplay, and you were snoring.

—I wasn't snoring. I was grunting.

She hoists up her skirt. It's plaid. High school colours.

—Snoring does not sound like grunting. You were talking in your sleep.

—Shelly, give me a break, I was… wait… what did I say?

She gives me a look. It's like a crack in a pipe, that look. The kind where dirty, poisonous things drip out and spoil everything.

—You were talking about someone.

Now I'm curious. —And…? Tell me more.

—Yes. Simon, I believe it was. Shelly narrows her eyes.

—You're gay, aren't you?

—What?

She's murmuring to herself as she stuffs something into her purse.

I am on my feet and my hand is on her shoulder.

—Come on, this is crazy. I sort of half-register that I'm naked and back off, vulnerable.

Shelly's coat is on, and she doesn't even tie her shoelaces. She's fumbling with the latch on the door.

—You were really good, you know, I say, unsure at this point what I'm trying to salvage. My integrity, I suppose.

—Billy, she says, enunciating. —Fuck. Off.

And she's gone.

I grab a cushion from the couch and place it over my cock and peep out the door. —Shelly, I call to her as she reaches the end of the hall and punches the elevator button. —We can just skip the foreplay and go right to sex if you want.

I race inside as various things from her purse shoot down the hall towards me. As I slam the door, she's screaming at me.

A crack of light widens at the far end of the living room, and my mother emerges from her bedroom, rubbing her eyes. —What the hell is all the noise? she's saying.

I dive over the couch, hiding amongst the cushions.

—Wait, Mom. I'm not decent.

—What the fuck are you doing to my couch?

I scramble towards my bedroom, hugging close to the ground.

I lock the door, ignoring my mom's demands that I explain. I pull on some track pants and I can hear her saying how that girl shouldn't be coming over here this late.

—What are you doing hanging around with her, anyway? She's not spouse material. What happened to that girl you went to Italy with?

I slump onto my bed, humiliated. —Mom, this is, um, sort of a bad time.

—What's wrong with you, Billy? says the door. —You smoke, you don't eat properly, you stay up all night, you fool around with a different girl every week, and you are flunking out of school. Are you on drugs?

—Spare me, okay? It's been a really bad day and I don't have the energy left for a long discussion with you about who is or *isn't* spouse material.

I'm yelling at a door.

—And I'm not gay! I say, throwing my pillow across the room.

Eventually the pounding at the door falls silent, except for a dry flapping sound. I slip into the bathroom. In the lava glow of the lightbulb I swallow some blue pills from the cabinet and splash water on my sallow face.

My face is a mountain the colour of ash.

From out of the Belly

When Mama comes home, I cry.

Tuesday night; her euchre night. The mingling scents of *crème de menthe* and lady's slims. The local housewives' clique — whom she lovingly calls her *curia hostilia* — have gathered once again.

"Oh, baby," she coos from the other room. "I'm back." The screen door whines shut behind her as she reaches down and one after another slips off her evening shoes. I wail my stuffing out. I can actually hear her holding her bloated belly by the sound of her hesitant shuffle as she comes to my rescue.

I shriek.

"Here I am!" she says, entering as a procession: her popped-out belly button, her unborn, then herself. The trinity that is Mama.

She scoops me out of my crib and coddles me. She pats my back. My wails turn to sniffles and hiccups.

"There, there," she says. "I'm sorry, munchkin. You must be starving, huh?"

Holding me in one arm, she prepares a bottle and stuffs it in my mouth. It is saltier than usual, but it is warm and comforting. She shifts her considerable weight and grumbles. After some time she begins to snore, and the bottle, long empty, falls away. I squeal again and she jolts awake, clutching her belly.

"Goddamit," she peers down at me, grabbing my arm and yanking me up. As she unceremoniously carries me back to bed, I wonder if Daddy will be home soon.

Mama drops me into the crib.

"Now quit crying and go to sleep," she says, then winces. Her hand is on her belly again. "Not a peep. Himself is kicking up a bad fuss tonight, and I don't need you making my headache worse."

She hovers in the near dark. A cold glitter where I know her eyes to be turns away. Then she is gone. Off to will her belly to sleep. He kicks up a fury; he makes her do things she regrets. 'Her little interloper,' she never neglects to mention. The prenatal pissant wins priority over me on all occasions, winnowing her loyalties (not to mention her marbles). The unborn bastard is the *linea negra* that divides us.

In the next room, Mama slips into a troubled sleep.

My attempt to drink in the morning sunlight spilling over the begonias is aborted as Mama stands to answer the phone. She lifts the handset off the wall cradle, her belly imposing itself between me and sun. From the shadows, I listen to her conversation.

"Hello?" A pause. Then she turns slightly away, possibly so that I can't read her lips, and she mutters: "No, I can't talk. I'm busy. *Because I have nothing to say.*"

I have a suspicion that Daddy is on the phone. I wonder where he's staying. Mama says he crawled away. It's so hard to tell if she's serious sometimes.

Mama continues, her voice rising: "Because you're a good-for-nothing, unkempt, vile, salacious little troll and I'll not have you anywhere near Simon or myself!" She hangs up, and not politely.

Mama stands rigid, seething below her wiry bangs. Then she composes herself and pivots on her heel to face me. For a moment, a faint promise of sunlight flashes, but she steps forward and eclipses me again. My head slumps forward and whacks my food tray despondently.

"Oops. Here we go," Mama says, lifting me back up to a sitting position. "You're all right." She rubs my head.

"Oh, *look*," she says, reaching across the tray and plucking something off the table. "It's Mr. Puppet!"

She slips her hand into the listless puppet and it springs to life. I like this game, so I laugh and stare. "Say hello, Mr. Puppet!"

"*Hello*," says Mr. Puppet.

Mama is good at voices. She explained to me once how she does this. Ventriloquism, she told me, wasn't what everyone else thought it was. Most people think it's a way for funny people to cast their voices and make it look like a smart-aleck puppet is telling all the good jokes.

But Mama told me what *really* happens is that someone who has very good listening and speaking skills—like super 20-20 hearing and a silky, razor-sharp voice, the kind that could convince rainbows to tie themselves into knots and convince snakes to eat their own tails—those people are able to talk to the spirits of the dead.

They need perfect hearing, because the dead drift along, not making very much noise at all, just the gentlest of hums and sighs. And when they hear them, they use their sweet-talking tongues to compel the dead to speak.

The voice is amplified by the special person's belly, otherwise nobody else would be able to hear what the dead say. Each spirit's voice is different, and quite colourful—who would have thought that unquiet spirits actually have a plethora of entertaining voices. Many have recurring roles. This one for instance; it is raspy, like two elderly hands rubbing sand between them. It always returns to do the voice for Mr. Puppet.

"How are you, Mr. Puppet?"

Mr. Puppet has curly black hair, a red nose, a purple shirt, and black eyes. Shark's eyes.

"*We are angry.*"

Mama frowns and looks from me to Mr. Puppet. "Why are you angry?"

"*Because Daddy is a loser. Daddy is no good. Daddy drinks a lot and spends all his time down at The Frisky Firkin with the pretty young waitresses when he should be at home doing his part around the house.*"

Mama feigns shock, but I can see right through that. I'm sure she's probably bubbling with enthusiastic froth, having found someone of the same mind as her—albeit a knitted hand puppet channeling the disembodied voice of the unquiet dead.

Mr. Puppet ends his cackling tirade and silently jerks a few times. If you don't interact with Mr. Puppet for a while, he twitches and struggles, as though trying to loose himself into the world. Mama senses his disquiet, and redirects the conversation.

"What have you done today, Mr. Puppet?" Mama asks.

"*We've been to the park,*" says Mr. Puppet.

Mama squints. "Now, Mr. Puppet. It isn't nice to fib. You couldn't have gone to the park. You have no legs."

Mr. Puppet is silent for a moment, looking at me with his black eyes. "*We've been to the park,*" says Mr. Puppet again.

"Okay, then," says Mama. "If you've been to the park, how did you get there? Did someone take you?" Mama smiles at me and winks, sure she has caught Mr. Puppet in a fib. Mama hates fibbers. I never fib because I can't talk yet. I wonder if Lord Bellykicker—may he choke on his meconium—will fib? The little bugger.

"*We crawled,*" says Mr. Puppet. "*We pulled our self with our arms. We even got run over when we crossed the street, and it hurrrrrrrrt...*"

Wow, Mr. Puppet is quite the Chatty Cathy today.

"I think we'd like to hear a different story..." Mama says.

"*...and when we finally got to the park we slithered through the dirt until we found our mommy...*"

"Okay then, that's quite enough out of you—"

Mr. Puppet shivers.

"*She was covered with dirt and so cold...*"

"That's enough, I said! You speak when I want you to speak!" Mama tears Mr. Puppet off her hand and throws him across the kitchen. Just then, the runt gives her a kick. I see her belly wobble from the inside. It must get her in the bladder, because she dashes off to the bathroom.

I watch Mr. Puppet, upside down on the floor. I want to hear more about the park, and I make noises that I think Mr. Puppet might understand, but it just lies there, soulless and empty, now that Mama is gone.

Mama comes stomping down the hallway.

"Stop it!" she cries. "Stop that crying!"

I hadn't been, but since she's in earshot now, and since she's scaring me, I whimper. The door of my room bursts open.

"You pathetic little shit!" she says. She always says this, and I don't really believe she means it. "Always crying, always begging."

I stop whimpering because I know she can't give me what I need. All I will get is a heartless cuddle and a bottle of salty milk.

"What have you got to say for yourself? Hmm? Nothing, eh? Can't talk, can you? No, you'll talk when I want you to."

I blink up at her. Normally I'm pretty forgiving of her wretched mood swings. I can take abuse, but everyone has their limit, and I've reached mine. In her truancy I've searched for my voice and found venom. I glare up from my cradle and say, "Mama, you're not being very kind." It isn't a yell, it isn't even a growl; just a simple statement, laced with what nuance of vitriol my tiny voice can produce. Nonetheless, Mama staggers backward, her face slack with shock.

"You…"

"Hush now," I say. "I've had just about enough out of you. You might be able to get away with talking to Mr. Puppet this way, but I think I deserve a little more effort on your part."

She stutters, scratching her head. She looks nervous.

"I don't ask much. Food, company, encouragement. It's not like I require taking for a walk. I certainly don't need fancy dinners. Just some attention. Some comfort when I cry. I don't blame you. I know you're tired and shaken and emotionally distraught, what with Daddy having left us the way he did, but you can't lose sight of your priorities, can you? Letting all this get to you is, well… it's the same as giving up. Think of what it's doing to me."

Mama whimpers, nibbling on her thumbnail.

"Give me a little assistance here," I say. "Help me want to be just like you when I grow up."

Just then there comes a persistent knocking at the front door. Mama wipes her eyes, gives me a final look, then hurries off to see who has come.

I hear her footsteps cross the living room. I hear the lock unbolt and the handle jiggle. Someone speaks. A woman. She says hello and introduces herself, but I cannot make out what she is saying. They seem to be arguing.

Then I hear footsteps and the person is in the house.

"I really don't see what all this fuss is about," Mama says.

"I understand your concern, Mrs. Willow, but it is important that you cooperate with me."

"I'm cooperating. But I fail to see why someone would call. Perhaps it was a misunderstanding? If you could just tell me who it was that made the complaint, I might be able to clarify what happened..."

"I'm sorry, but, as I'm sure you must realize, I cannot divulge privileged information."

"But—"

"Mrs. Willow, if I could just see your child."

"I don't think that's necessary..."

"I wouldn't want to come back with the police to convince you, as that tends to make things awfully unpleasant. Come now, Mrs. Willow. It won't take long."

"He's sleeping," says Mama.

"I understand, and I won't make a peep."

Mama protests again, but then footsteps are coming down the hall, and quietly the door opens, and a dark shape stands in the crack of light.

A woman with a clipboard enters. She has her hair drawn tight into a black bun, and her face is partially in shadow. She moves closer to the crib. Leans in.

I knew this would happen eventually.

The woman with the clipboard touches my face, then, drawing back, she flicks the light on, grabs me by the foot and lifts me up into the air.

"Mrs. Willow," she says, sounding nonplussed. "What is the meaning of this? Where is your child?" She shakes me.

I hear Mama's voice out in the living room. She speaks softly. "He's in his crib, sleeping."

"There is only a doll here. I'll ask you again," She steps into the hall and holds me up. The curly black string that is my hair dangles like a mop head. "Where is Simon?"

I wonder what will become of Mr. Puppet when this is all said and done? Will he cease to exist? Will whoever it is that moves in and takes him over simply sink back into the void?

Mama says something I don't catch, and the woman tenses. She gasps, dropping her clipboard, clapping a hand over her face. She turns to flee. There is something odd about Mama's voice. It has not come from the dark space in the middle of that mass of black hair, but from her gut. And the voice is deep. Like Daddy's.

I sit in my highchair, waiting.

Mama sits on the kitchen floor, holding her belly. He is kicking hard now, and she's sweating, clenching her jaw.

I sing softly for her. She doesn't comment, but hopefully it soothes her. She throws her head back. It's time.

The little bastard is coming at last.

Hours of Wealth

The electronics store closed at eleven p.m., and it was ten minutes to when Darrell pulled up and hurried across the parking lot, holding the video camera in his hand. He had no idea which cables would do what he wanted, so he asked an employee for help. He was given a generic cable that cost twenty dollars, and he rushed through the checkout. As he left the store, he popped out the LCD screen on the video camera and hit play, watching the home movie he'd discovered as he crossed the parking lot to his car.

The DV cassette had been stuffed in beside old VHS tapes labeled "soaps" and "game shows." Darrell hadn't recognized it, and thought it might have belonged to another family member, since his parents had never owned a DV cam, as far as he knew. The rest of the contents of the box were ruined. The tapes had looked old and warped by age and moisture. But the DV cassette was in a plastic case, and when he had opened it there hadn't been any sign of wear or deterioration. He'd put the cassette in his front shirt pocket and slid the box aside.

The tape had been playing for more than three hours now, probably a result of extended play mode. He remembered that on some VHS tapes you could get six or sometimes eight hours on one tape. He wasn't sure how long DV cassettes went, though. The time index down in the corner of the screen said 7058:10:50. It seemed to be counting upwards accurately. He had indeed watched only a couple of hours since he'd purchased the video camera at a pawn shop downtown.

In his apartment he plugged the red and white cables into the back of the camera, and on the back of his VCR he plugged the other end into the AUX IN jack. He switched the set on and flipped to the *input* channel. He pressed play on the camera, and an image of an infant appeared on his twenty-seven-inch screen, and the sound was clear and loud. At the pawn shop, when he first tested it, the video had seemed dark and muffled. He placed the camera on the floor in front of the television set and sat down on the couch.

Rose, his mother, was singing lovingly to the baby that he knew must be himself, but with whom he strangely he had trouble associating. He stopped fidgeting with the camera at that point and elected to just watch the tape for a while to see what else was on it.

An hour later both mom and baby had fallen asleep, and Darrell was beginning to wonder if maybe his dad had fallen asleep at the controls too, since the video just showed them sleeping. It went on and on, and Darrell was sure the tape would run out. But it didn't, and after a while the baby began to cry and his mom woke up. She was breastfeeding the hungry infant when the unexpected occurred.

The tape went blurry and auto-refocused again, and then his father walked into frame, carrying flowers. For a moment, Darrell was confused. If Dad was just coming in now, who was holding the camera? As his dad set the flowers on the bedside table and kissed his wife, then leaned down and kissed the baby, it occurred to Darrell that he didn't greet whoever was holding the camera.

It went on like that. Dad sat on the edge of the bed and talked in a low voice with Darrell's mother. He couldn't make out what they were saying. The whole time the image didn't move. It was then that he realized the obvious. Dad had set the camera down on some surface in the hospital room and left it there so that mom and baby could have a nap, perhaps not knowing that it was still recording.

"I hope you didn't throw anything out that I would have wanted to keep," said Rose over the phone.

"No, Mom, nothing that wasn't completely ruined. Most of the stuff lower down was sitting in water for days. It was a mess. Lots of the boxes had turned to mush."

"That really is too bad. I've been meaning to go through that stuff for years now. I guess it's too late."

"Well, even after I'm done there's still plenty there to sort through. You should really think about clearing that space out, Mom."

"One of these days. Thank you for doing this, though. It's a big help. Your father can't lift all that stuff with his back and everything, and all the damp and mildew would just be the death of me."

"Not a problem. So hey, you never told me you had home videos, Mom," Darrell said into the phone. In the background, the image was still going. He was impressed with the length of the tape. It had been playing for nearly four hours straight and hadn't stopped yet, but he expected it to soon.

"What do you mean?" his mom was saying.

"There's a tape from a camcorder that has me as a baby. Looks like we're at the hospital."

"Where?"

"I have it here, I'm watching now. You're breastfeeding me again. Jesus I was a hungry kid…"

"Are you sure? I don't…"

"Mom, it's you. You're only about twenty-three in the video, but it's you. Dad's on it, too, but he didn't stay for long. He brought you flowers…"

"… Where did you find that?" she sounded confused.

"There was a box in your storage space. Had a bunch of water-damaged VHS tapes in it. This was between the ruined tapes, but it was fine. It plays."

"I remember that."

"The tape?" Darrell asked.

"No… I remember your father bringing me flowers after you were born. He was still working at the department store and he couldn't stay for the visiting hours, but he came with flowers…"

"So it is from my birth. I knew it."

"We never owned a video camera, though…"

"Maybe you borrowed one and forgot. Besides, I think someone left the camera on a table or something and forgot about it. It doesn't move, it just sort of stays focused on us in the hospital room. I'm sure the tape probably just runs out with us breastfeeding or something… I haven't gotten to the end yet, though."

"Hold on a sec, Darrell…" he heard the phone muffle up, and his mom called his father. He heard her ask him if he remembered shooting any baby videos. He could hear his father's typical short response. "Nup…"

"Darrell, Dad says he never made any baby videos."

"Well, someone did, Mom, I'm watching it right now."

"That's so odd…" she trailed off. "… Are you sure it's me?"

"Positive."

"So strange…"

"Ma," Darrell said before he hung up.

"Huh?"

"You were beautiful."

She was quiet for a moment. Then, "What do you mean *were*?" They laughed. Then she said, "Thank you, Darrell."

"Love you," he said.

"Love you, too."

Darrell was home still; it was one o'clock the following day. He'd stayed up all night, and called into work sick. Shelley, a girl at work he had been seeing for over a month, had called to ask if he was okay.

"Yeah, I'll be all right. Just not feeling well today."

"Too bad," she said. "I guess you'd better stay in tonight."

"Hmm? Oh right, the movie. Yeah, I'm sorry, we can do it maybe on the weekend?"

Her voice rose in pitch, noticeably trying not to sound disappointed. "Oh it's okay, totally. Whenever you feel better. I just hope you aren't sick of me already."

"Of course I'm not," Darrell said.

"I miss you," she said suddenly. Then added, "I mean, not in like some weird way or anything."

He sensed that she couldn't talk freely. Someone was probably standing near her. Maybe Doug, the manager.

"Listen, I better go…"

"Doug is standing there, isn't he?"

"Well no, but almost," she said.

"Yeah. You're right, he just wouldn't understand."

"Ex*actly*," she had this way of smiling with her tone of voice that made him feel jittery.

"Okay, hope it isn't too busy for you today."

"It'll be fine. You better be back in tomorrow, though."

"Yeah?" Darrell said. "Or else what?"

"You wish," she said.

Darrell resumed the tape. It had not run out yet, having gone for nearly twenty-four hours straight, and it was still going. He had even fast-forwarded through large sections. How there could possibly be that much tape in one little cassette was inexplicable, but there it was.

What had started off as a video of him and his mother in hospital, shortly after his birth, had become something infinitely stranger. His mom had been in the hospital for one night and had gone home the next day. The camera didn't turn off the entire time. Whether they slept or breastfed or entertained visitors, the camera stayed fixed. If someone picked baby Darrell up and moved him out of view, the camera moved to keep him in frame.

When they were eventually discharged from the hospital, the camera lifted from whatever surface it had been sitting on and went with them down the hall, outside into the sunlight, across the sidewalk and into the waiting car. The frame stayed on him, pointing at the infant strapped into his car seat, during the trip home.

Darrell fast-forwarded the tape for hours and hours, stopping it at places, sometimes at random, sometimes when he saw something interesting. Here he was breastfeeding again, here he was crying while Mom changed his newborn diapers. He fast-forwarded through what appeared to be his entire first day home, and through the night, baby waking up every few hours or less to be fed or changed.

When he slept and the lights went out, the camera couldn't focus properly and would go blurry, but whenever he started crying again a dim nightlight would wink on and it would be just enough for the image to autofocus and there he would be, small and pink and weeping and getting fed. It gave him chills at the idea of someone staying up all night in a dark room filming a sleeping baby. What chilled him further was that no one on the tape ever acknowledged the person behind the camera.

Darrell decided to stop the tape and try fast-forwarding it that way, since it seemed to go much faster. He pressed the FF button on the side of the camera and the motor clicked and he could hear the tape heads spinning ahead. He had no idea how far to go, or how much tape was speeding by, but he stopped it after counting to twenty.

He pressed play.

The image came back. He was crawling, and Mom was rolling a ball towards him. Baby Darrell laughed. The time code at the bottom read 11426:22:43.

All at once he realized that the numbers at the bottom weren't wrong at all. It was the correct time—in hours. Darrell's skin prickled. For a moment he didn't think about how impossible this seemed, and tried to calculate in his head. 11,426 hours... over a year. Maybe a year and a half. The television screen glowed against his face, the baby on it making happy mumbling noises. He had no real experience with babies, but he felt sure that eighteen-month-old children were much more developed than this. Baby Darrell here was much younger than a year and a half…

Unless…

Darrell felt his stomach go cold, as if he'd swallowed an ice cube. He stopped the tape, and his finger hovered over the rewind button.

"I just can't imagine where these videos came from," said Rose Joyce, watching the tape Darrell had brought over, showing some scenes he'd copied from the original.

On the television, baby Darrell was eating a spaghetti noodle with his fingers, his face covered in sauce.

He hadn't told his mother the extent of the tape. She knew only that there were a lot of baby videos, and that she had no recollection of them ever being filmed. Rose had insisted that they had never owned or even borrowed a camcorder, and that it was a quiet regret she'd kept for many years. But here there were videos after all, and soon she forgot her confusion over the origin of the tape and simply enjoyed watching the antics of baby Darrell.

Darrell hadn't gone back to the beginning of the tape, afraid of what he would see. But he had gone forward a bit before he'd left the house with about an hour of randomly selected bits copied onto VHS. He had fast-forwarded the tape for about a minute and a half and when he'd pressed play the time code had been at 27468:40:42. Darrell had used a calculator to discover that, minus the approximately forty-two weeks of possibly prenatal video, he had been just over two years old and sleeping in his crib in nothing but a diaper. There had been a small nightlight in the room, but it had done little to illuminate him. The streetlights from outside had cast an outline of blue-white around him. For many minutes Darrell had watched himself sleeping. He'd imagined that his parents were likely sleeping at that moment on the tape, too. He'd left the tape running when he'd left his apartment.

Darrell looked at his mother now and searched her face for the younger woman she once was. Her hands fidgeted in her lap as she watched a clip of her, Darrell and his father, Edwin, at a park.

"Oh, that's Morningside Park!" Rose said, nodding to herself. "We used to go there all the time when you were a baby. We had to stop going there because a bee landed on you and scared the daylights out of you."

"I was stung?" Darrell asked. On the tape, baby Darrell had on a blue sunhat and was waddling around in the grass. In the background he could see his father in a lawn chair, reading a book.

"No, it didn't sting you. But it sure upset you. You cried and cried. We brought you back a few times after that but you wouldn't have any of it. Your dad didn't believe you could recognize the park. Said all parks looked the same to a two-year-old. But you had a tantrum whenever we went there, so we stopped going."

When the tape ended, Rose sighed.

"Those were good days," she said. "Funny how it all comes back."

"I don't recognize any of it. My earliest memories are from I think four or five. I remember camping and kindergarten and that sort of thing."

"What else is on the tape?" she asked.

Darrell hadn't told her that the tape was continuous and unwavering, minute by minute, every day, seven days a week.

"I don't know. I haven't watched it all yet. A lot, I think."

Rose shook her head. "It's so strange. These sorts of recorders weren't around in the seventies. We didn't have much money then, either. You were our big expense," she said to him and smiled.

"You don't think it might have been Uncle Joe or someone? Or maybe a friend?" Darrell didn't believe it even as he suggested it. The only thing more impossible than a continuous tape that seemed to start in the womb and follow you around 24/7 through infancy without any jumps, cuts or edits was the idea that someone had filmed it. But if someone hadn't been there filming it… then where had it come from?

She shook her head. "No, I don't recall anybody filming these sorts of things. There are videos of some family weddings floating around, but that's all."

"Ma," he said after a moment filled with bewildered silence.

"What is it?" she asked, seeing his serious expression.

He was going to ask if she believed in the supernatural, but he decided not to. Instead, he said, "Nothing. I should really get going. I have stuff I need to do."

"Okay. Well, thanks for bringing that tape over. You sure you don't mind if I keep this tape? I'd like to watch it again."

"Of course. I mixed these clips together for you."

When Darrell left his mother's house a cool breeze had picked up and he rubbed his arms as he walked to his dark car.

When he got home the tape was still on, as he expected it would be, and baby Darrell was still sleeping.

There was a message on his phone from Shelley. "I tried calling you on your cell but all I got was your voicemail. I uh, hope you are feeling better and stuff. Um… so when you get back give me a call if you want." The last part had a very noticeable confused and hurt sound in it and he cursed himself. She of course had thought he was home sick. He felt terrible, imagining what she must be thinking. It was strange, the guilt. He'd only been seeing her for five or six weeks and already worried about what she thought of him. Relationships had never moved that fast for him. He felt... attached to Shelley.

He dialed her number and waited as it rang once, twice three times. She picked up and for a moment he heard a television show in the background, but it went quiet when she said, "Hello?" into the phone.

"Hey, you," he said, trying to sound like he wasn't worried.

"Oh, hey," she said, in an equally nonchalant voice, neither too eager, nor too concerned.

"I'm glad you're there," he said. "I just got back from my mother's house. She needed me to fix her VCR," he cringed, hoping this didn't sound lame.

"She got an old one?" Shelley asked.

"Yeah. It eats tapes. I keep telling her to buy a new one but she never throws anything away."

"That's too funny," Shelley said. "So... how are you feeling?"

"Better, actually. Which is why I'm calling."

"You mean you weren't just calling because you missed my voice so much and couldn't stand to not talk with me for another minute?"

"Well, that too," Darrell said. "But I also called to see if you wanted to come over."

She giggled to herself. The discomfort seemed to have vanished from her voice. "It's kinda late. What do you want to do?"

"Fool around?" he said before he could think better of it.

She laughed a good throaty laugh. "I can't believe you just said that."

He was laughing too. "Just kidding," he said. "Sort of."

She laughed again. He could hear her breath puffing into the phone. "Yeah, okay weirdo," she said.

"But seriously. We could watch a movie here if you want."

"Well I'd love to," Shelley said. "But I do have to get up for an appointment in the morning. Why don't we plan to rent a movie on Friday?"

"Oh. Okay, sure. That sounds good," Darrell said. Then he added, "You know I wasn't really serious, right?"

"Hmm?"

"About fooling around…"

She burst into laughter again. "You're cute. But are you saying you *don't* want to fool around with me?"

They talked for another half hour before she finally had to go. "So don't go getting sick on Friday. You're all mine."

"I'll never get sick again."

"And if your mother's VCR breaks… too bad. She can wait until Sunday."

"I thought it was just Friday?"

"The movie might go late," she said. "I might have to stay over."

Darrell laughed, but his heart was pounding. "Well, better bring your pajamas then."

"I don't wear pajamas…" she said. "Bye, Darrell."

Darrell meant to go to bed at a decent hour, but he couldn't take his attention off images playing on the screen. He watched it deep into the night, until his heavy eyes couldn't hold themselves open any more. He fell asleep to the sound of his own toddler voice babbling away, the blue flickering television light casting mushrooms of shadow across the walls, playing on his face, slipping, receding, falling.

Darrell pulled up to the house he shared with his landlady, who lived upstairs. He had a separate side entrance to his basement apartment. He shut off the ignition and stepped wearily from the car, and to his surprise saw Shelley sitting on the step in front of his door.

"Hey," she said, putting away a novel she'd been reading.

"Hey... what are you doing here?"

"I dunno. I thought I'd come over," she said, standing, approaching.

"I thought we were doing something on Friday?" He said.

"Yeah," she said. "But I thought I could steal a few hours with you," and she kissed him, her hands cupping his face; framing him. Seeing him.

At four in the morning, just hours after Shelley had left, Darrell discovered the bee incident. Baby Darrell didn't immediately notice the bee land on his leg, but then he started screaming. The insect flew away and a little bead of blood welled up in the spot where it had been. His mother and father were with him now, picking him up. The spot on his leg had become red and swollen and his father was leaning in, inspecting it, but baby Darrell's legs were kicking and he was wailing.

"But there was nobody else there," his mother said.

"I mean, I just don't see how you could forget a trip to the hospital with a swollen, bee-stung toddler," Darrell said.

"I just never saw any sense in telling you about it. We don't like to talk about hospital things," she said.

"What do you mean?"

"Let's not go into that. I just don't understand this whole tape business. There was nobody with us. And I'm absolutely certain that nobody followed us into the hospital room with a video camera. They would never have been allowed in."

"I know, Mom. I… I can't explain it…"

"What else is on this tape?"

He took a deep breath. "Mom…"

"I mean, what if some weirdo was filming us without our knowledge… there are people like that, you know…"

"Mom…listen."

"Do you think that someone broke into the storage space and put the tape there? Maybe you shouldn't go back…"

"Mom, please listen," Darrell said, raising his voice. "The tape has a lot more on it."

"Like what else? They didn't film me in the shower or anything, did they?"

"No, Mom. But there's more on there."

"What?"

He sighed. "Everything."

She was silent for a moment. Then: "I don't understand. Did you say…"

"The tape has everything on it."

"What are you talking about?"

Darrell told her. Naturally, she didn't believe him.

"Why would you say something like that…"

"I'm not making it up. Listen, are you going to be home later?"

"Of course," she said, sounding anxious and angry.

"Okay, after work I'm bringing the tape over. I want to show you."

"Don't be ridiculous, I have to…"

"I need to show you. I need to show someone else. I can't keep this to myself any more."

Rose Joyce was weeping, and her hand was over her mouth. Darrell looked at her for a moment, and then back at the television screen. The picture on it was immediately after his birth. He was being cleaned by nurses, and his skin was mottled. His face was twisted up and he was wailing. He had risked rewinding the tape and, mercifully, it had gone back smoothly.

Together, Darrell and his mother had watched as patches of light appeared on the screen, and muffled sounds, and suddenly a crack of light and the camera seemed to follow baby Darrell out of the birth canal into the harsh light of the delivery room. The moment the infant took its first breath and began to scream, Darrell choked back his own tears.

Baby Darrell was swaddled and given to his weeping mother, and he paused the tape. The frozen image was of him with a squinty, sort of unhappy expression, but his mother's expression was one of exhausted joy.

Rose was shaking.

"Mom?"

She looked at him. "What are we watching? It's not some prank, is it?"

"Of course not."

"How is this possible?"

Before now he'd still thought of it as a sort of candid home video with some kind of reasonable explanation attached to it. But when the camera was inside his mother and actually emerged with the baby, his mind reeled with disbelief.

Darrell decided not to show his mother any more of the tape, and he stopped it.

"What are you doing?" she said.

"That's probably enough for today, don't you think?"

She was quiet, staring at the blank television screen. Then she nodded.

Darrell packed up the camera and the cords and put his coat and shoes on.

"Does it really go on?"

"Yeah," he said. "I've been watching it all week and I got up to about three years old."

"Holy Jesus," she said. "Without stopping?"

"I fast-forwarded it a lot, but all the parts I saw were consistent. It never stops. It follows me, every minute of every day, even when I'm sleeping or in the tub."

She started to cry again.

"Are you scared?" she asked.

"Of course," Darrell said. "But I'm excited, too. I'm experiencing my life again. Witnessing the parts I was too young to remember. Like the bee sting."

She sniffled. "I'm sorry I never told you the truth about that. I just..."

"You don't like to talk about hospital things, I know."

Rose shook her head. "Well, that's part it. You scared us. The swelling seemed so bad, we—your father and I—we thought you might not make it. When the doctor said you'd be fine we were so relieved. I didn't ever want anyone to know I thought you were dying."

Darrell had just watched the tape and he knew that he hadn't actually swelled up at all. The sting was red, but that was about it. He didn't mention this to his mother, though.

"I overreacted," she said. "When you have your own child, don't rush it off to the hospital every time it gets the sniffles. People will think you're a lunatic."

"I don't think you're a lunatic. And I don't know a single person who does."

She laughed and hugged him.

"I'd like to see more," she said after a few minutes.

"Well maybe I'll come back over in a few days and we'll watch more."

"On the weekend?" she asked.

"How about Sunday?"

"That would be fine."

"Will you be all right?"

"Oh, yes," she said. Then she cast her eyes down. "I suppose this whole bit with me crying will be on the tape now. I mean… it's still being made right now, isn't it?"

A cold tongue of discomfort pushed across his flesh.

"I hadn't thought of that," he said. The hair on his arms felt electric. "I'm not sure."

"You should check. Zip through it and see how far it goes. Maybe there's some ghost floating around with a camera right now as we speak."

That night Darrell fast-forwarded his life. Through his infancy a second time, then his toddler years went by, then his pre-teens. He would sit with his finger hovering over the stop button. He went five and sometimes ten minutes at a time, for hours, stopping and pressing play to check the status, keeping a log in a notebook of the time codes with a brief description of events and his estimated age. He stopped more often on instances of himself sleeping or sitting in class than anything else. One embarrassing moment came when he stopped the tape somewhere in his early teens and discovered himself in the bathroom masturbating. After this, scenes of him using the washroom lost their humiliating effects. It hit him again and again, things he'd forgotten about.

It occurred to Darrell that his various girlfriends would be on the tape, and he was suddenly determined to find the day he lost his virginity. It had been with a girl from school. He had been fifteen, her fourteen. It had been in the months before summer, perhaps in May. He tried to get his bearings as to when he was, and decided that the easiest way was to calculate what the time code would be in May of his fourteenth year, 1987. He multiplied the hours over fourteen years and came up with the number 129360.

The time code was currently 128998:02:01.

The image was of him playing Nintendo games. He timed himself and found that it took about ten minutes to go through an entire day. It went much faster than that when fast-forwarding with the image off. The time code seemed to advance about one year in less than ten minutes. When he'd reached what he thought was his fourteenth year, he increased the intervals he checked the tape at. It was winter, but likely after Christmas. Then the snow was gone, but he still wore a coat outside. Then the coat became a lighter jacket.

When he reached what he was positive was May of 1987, he left the visual scanning on and just watched his days go by. Again he marveled at how often he seemed to be sleeping or in school. He also laughed at how often he masturbated.

It all seemed so routine, as though the same day kept repeating itself. He saw the same places, the same people, the same sorts of things again and again. Weekends were no different, except that he wasn't watching himself sitting through classes. He played it now and then to see certain things, like what he was watching on television at the time, or to hear a conversation he was having with a friend (to which he usually laughed in embarrassment at how juvenile he sounded). He watched with raised eyebrows at a fight he'd gotten into after school. He'd lost.

Darrell was beginning to wonder if he'd remembered the time of year incorrectly when all of a sudden he found what he was looking for. He hit the play button and there he was, with her. She'd had red hair. Rachel was her name. They were walking along a street near the house he'd lived in as a teenager. They were flirting with each other. He was visibly more nervous than she was.

They stepped into a small grove of trees near a children's playground. He was holding her hand. It was the afternoon, and the sun pierced the trees in shafts. They had skipped class to come here. Rachel kept asking if this was a good spot, and teenaged Darrell kept wondering if maybe they should go deeper in. Eventually they found a spot, and there was an awkward, stiff kiss. She put her tongue in his mouth, he remembered, but on the tape he saw only their jaws moving around, and their faces pressed together. Fumbling for purchase. Hesitating. His eyes were closed and his face upturned, lit by sunlight. His hands were on her hips. Her hands were on his face. He was all hands and fingers. She was all eyes and kisses.

Darrell copied this, and more, onto tapes, grouping them together and labeling them. Sexual interludes. Vacations. Drinking parties. Times he cried. Fights that he was humiliated to see again, understanding how ridiculously selfish he'd been. He felt like calling people and apologizing for things he watched himself say. Funerals and weddings. Graduation. Frosh week. Darrell went out and bought dozens of VHS tapes and over the next few days, between work and sleep, he filled them. Highlights of his life.

By Friday he had discovered the answer he'd set out looking for days ago after his mother had asked him how far the
tape went. As he watched his answer, he felt both nauseous
and exhilarated. On the screen, he was in his mother's storage
space, sifting through soggy junk. He watched himself find the
tape. Then everything went black and his heart stopped. He
turned up the sound. He could hear himself moving around,
and he remembered that the lights had been on a timer, and
had gone out on him several times. When the fluorescent lights
flared back on, the camera was up near the ceiling of the storage space and blurry, but it auto-refocused quickly and began
tracking him again, moving down from the ceiling and keeping him in a tight frame, from the waist up.

He pressed fast-forward.

"Hello?" he said into the phone after clearing his throat.
He'd paused the tape. On the screen, it was him and Shelley
the night she'd surprised him. Just a few nights ago. How this
was appearing on the tape he didn't know. He wasn't sure he
wanted to know. He found himself looking around with darting eyes, trying to spot the camera filming his life, but he was
alone.

"Hey!" It was Shelley. He looked at her on the screen, and
listened to her on the phone.

"Well, hello there," he said, remembering that it was Friday
and that she was coming over.

"So, I'm hungry… do you want to go get something to
eat first?"

"Yes," he said. "I'm starving. And I need to get out of the
house."

"You alright?" asked Shelley.

"Yeah. Just strung out. I've had a lot of work to do here and I'm sick of looking at it."

"Oh, like boring work stuff, or interesting work stuff?"

He coughed, then said: "Oh, a little of both. I'll tell you about it later."

As he said it, he stopped the tape and the screen went black.

An hour later he picked her up and they went to an Italian restaurant for dinner.

Darrell thought about the tape all night. But he was also glad to be away from it. His life felt compressed. Telescoped. He was weary, his head pounding. Shelley kept asking if he felt alright, saying he looked pale. His answer was that he was tired, but that he felt better now that she was there.

After dinner they walked back to his apartment, pressing against a gusty wind that blew leaves and paper cups down the street. To the west, Darrell could see the glow of the city's downtown lights reflecting on craggy, low-hanging clouds.

"It's a good thing you're staying over," he said to Shelley. "It looks like it might rain."

She hooked her arm tighter around his and put her head against his shoulder.

"Wow," said Shelley, seeing the stacks of VHS tapes piled around his television set. "What's all that?"

"Oh, it's nothing," he said, wishing he'd had the foresight to tidy up before bringing her home. "It's just this thing I'm doing."

"Oh, yeah?" said Shelley, picking up one of the tapes. The label read *Summer-Fall '82*. "Sounds interesting."

"They're just some home movies. I'm compiling some stuff together for my mom."

"Oh, let's watch! I love home movies," Shelley said.

Darrell's stomach flipped. "Well, actually I've been staring at them for like two days straight, I'd really rather not right now..."

"Oh, come on," she said, giggling. She went over to the camcorder on top of the television set. "Got any cute baby movies or something?"

"I really don't," he started to say, but Shelley had pressed play on the camcorder, laughing.

The picture came on. There was moaning. Two bodies were writhing on a bed.

"Oh! Oh, I'm sorry..." she said. But then she stopped. Her expression went from embarrassment to confusion to shock. "Is that...?"

The scene on the television was Darrell's bedroom. Shelley's face was unmistakable underneath him, eyes closed, mouth opened, her legs hooked behind Darrell's back.

He saw in her eyes a mixture of horror and heartbreak.

"What is this?" she asked.

Darrell's heart was pounding. He could explain what the tape was, but she wouldn't believe him. He could of course prove it to her by showing what else was on the tape, but he wondered if she'd even stay around long enough to be convinced. To her it looked plain and simple. He had videotaped them. She stared around at all the VHS tapes, surely imagining the horrible things that might be on all of them.

"It's complicated," he said. "Do you want an explanation?"

Her face was flushed. "I don't understand... why would you do that?"

Darrell looked at her. "This isn't what you think it is, I promise,"

She looked around her, searching for her bag. "I think I should go."

"Do you want me to explain?" he asked again.

"I don't think so," she said, putting her shoes on.

He wanted her to get upset. To scream or cry. But she did neither. She just put her shoes on and took up her bag and went to the door, all in very purposeful, unstoppable movements. But she flashed him a look as she unlatched the door; a soiled look, and he realized that she was too humiliated to respond in any way other than to just leave without another word.

Darrell watched her walk up the street, the rain blowing sideways against her body, arms wrapped tightly around herself, her head down, hair hanging over her face like a burial cloth.

Darrell forwarded through the last couple of days, wanting to watch the incident that had just occurred. He wanted to see if it was there, somehow magically deposited on the tape as it occurred. Was there a lag time between real life and the tape? Did it record in real time?

Most of what he saw now was himself, sitting in front of the television, watching the DV. The scene changed only a few times. He didn't eat or sleep much. *No wonder I'm so tired,* he thought.

He scanned quickly through their dinner together. He frowned at their kisses, and handholding; their intimacy seemed stolen and obscene to him now.

If she had only stayed, he could have showed her all this and explained what the tape really was. She could still be here.

On the television, they were getting up and moving into the living room. Then they were standing in front of the screen, and it was happening. Through his bitter regret he still felt awe and a little fear that something so recent was on the tape already. He pressed fast-forward. She left quickly and he stood there for a while. Then he was sitting. Watching himself watch himself, caught in a hall of mirrors. He moved, and the other Darrell moved.

The camera angle was pointing down on him from up and to the left. He looked up, expecting to see a hole in the universe or something, but there was nothing there. He looked back at the television, and on the screen he saw himself look up at the camera, and Darrell felt utter dread. Then a weird sound came from the tape, and the image fluttered with black lines. When it became clear again, he was doing jumping jacks and laughing. He slowed the tape to normal playback speed and watched. On the screen, he was jumping up towards the camera, looking *right at it*, waving his arms.

Again he cast a quick glance up at the empty corner of the ceiling, feeling faint. Feeling like he needed to run or scream. Like he needed to get out the house. He felt watched. *Pursued.*

He shut off the tape and stood with his hand on his mouth. After a moment, he pressed play again, not believing what he saw. Then a moment of disorientation hit him. Despite a very slight delay, the tape was running in real time, the image on the screen doing exactly what he was doing, only a fraction of a second before. Darrell shivered uncontrollably. It felt as though he simply had the camera pointed at himself, watching as he taped his actions. He waved, he made faces. He stood and jumped up and down.

fast-forwarding into the future, he looked comical, jumping around and dancing. Then he saw himself sit down and talk on the phone. He set the playback to normal and turned up the volume, but he couldn't hear what he was saying. Then the onscreen Darrell hung up the phone. fast-forwarding further, he saw himself leave the house.

A few minutes later the phone rang.
"Is this Darrell," said a female voice.
"Yes. This is."
"Hi," said the angry sounding voice. "This is Kate. I'm a friend of Shelley's."
Oh shit.
"Oh, um hi," he said.
"Shelley won't let me involve the police, *or* my boyfriend, but I just wanted to let you know that if that sick tape of yours ends up on the internet or anything, I promise you that you'll have every bone in your body broken, you fucking pervert—" then she hung up.

Darrell didn't wake up until late on Saturday afternoon, but despite sleeping all day he didn't feel refreshed. He left the house without looking at the tape, getting on the subway and letting it take him downtown where he paid for a movie ticket to a comedy. When he realized he was too distracted to follow the story of the film, he got up and left. He wandered around the city streets and eventually went home.

Darrell fast-forwarded the tape, but didn't keep track of the time. In the end, he couldn't resist his gut curiosity to see something in the far future, but he distanced himself by not wanting to know exactly how far he was going.

He was jogging on a beach, looking much older. He wasn't the athletic type, and seeing himself jogging was disorienting.

Fast-forward.

He was on the toilet. Grey had appeared in his hair. There was a hideous scar on his chin.

Fast-forward.

He was at a crosswalk, holding a child's hand. Was it *his* child?

Fast-forward.

Sleeping.

On the toilet again.

Sleeping again.

Christmas. He opened a present. It was a camera. People he didn't recognize were sitting around him smiling and saying surprise. On the tape he was saying "Oh, my god, you shouldn't have gotten me this, it's so expensive!"

Fast-forward.

Fast-forward.

Suddenly there was a solemn scene. He was standing in a field, wearing a suit. His mother was in a wheelchair beside him on one side. On the other side of him was a woman, blonde, unfamiliar. Beside her, a teenaged girl. The sky was grey. In the background he could see rocks, all in a line. No, not rocks. Stones. They were in a graveyard.

A funeral.

A wave of icy fear fell on him.

Darrell didn't see his father in the scene. He could hear a eulogy being spoken in soft tones. His mother, old and looking very withered, was weeping.

He stopped the tape and fast-forwarded, not wanting to see. Not wanting to know.

Dad. The thought came to him despite his best efforts to suppress it.

The phone rang.

"Hello?" he answered, his hand shaking.

"Darrell."

It was his father.

"Hey, Dad. How's life?"

He felt like crying.

"Well, your mother's got a cough, but otherwise great." His responses were never about himself, when asked how he was. They were always about Rose. "Is your power out?"

"No. You have a blackout?" Darrell said.

"Yup. It's been out for five minutes or so. Looks like it's dark as far down as the Danforth. I thought I'd call and see if yours was out too."

"No, they're fine. Must be your grid or something."

"That's a pissoff, I was watching my show."

"Listen, Dad. Do you think I could come over for a while?"

"Well, we don't have any power. Are you sure that's how you want to spend your evening?"

"Yeah. Maybe we can play cards or something."

"Alright, when will you be here?"

"Give me about twenty minutes," Darrell said.

"Yup, see you."

Darrell hung up the phone. *It's a long way off,* he said to himself. The scene showed him much, much older. For all he knew it was still thirty years off. *Hell,* he thought. *It might not have been Dad.*

But somehow he knew that it was.

Suddenly there was a whining sound from the camera, and he realized that it was still fast-forwarding. The whine rose in pitch, and then, with a sound that made him jump, the tape stopped.

Darrell stared at the black television.

It had stopped.

He reached for the camera and pressed the fast-forward button again, but it just clicked and went silent.

The end of the tape had been reached.

He left the house, too afraid to touch the camera. Being close to it made him feel dead already. As he drove to his parent's house he couldn't shake the sound of the tape stopping. The sound of a coffin lid slamming shut.

As he entered his parents' neighbourhood, he felt an eerie sense of dread. All the houses were blackened and the stop signals and streetlamps were lifeless. His headlights seemed to be the only source of light. When he pulled up to the house he could see the shape of his father in the front window, silhouetted by flickering candlelight.

They sat at the dining room table. The cherry on the end of his father's cigarette glowed as he leaned in and lit it with the candle's flame.

"So what's bothering you?" his dad asked.

"Nothing, Dad. I was just bored."

Edwin Joyce nodded and tapped an ash off the end of his cigarette. "Whatever it is, it'll pass."

They were quiet for a moment. Outside, he could hear a cricket chirping.

"I wonder how long it'll last…" his dad said.

"The blackout?"

"Yup. They don't usually go this long."

"I'm sure it'll be back on soon enough," Darrell said, staring at the flame.

"They always scared you. When you were little, I mean."

Darrell looked up at his father's face, smoke drifting up in front of it like grey seaweed.

"Did they?" Darrell said.

"I remember you came out from your room one night when we had a blackout. You were maybe six or seven years old. You were crying and said you couldn't sleep because it was too dark. I tried to tell you that if you closed your eyes you wouldn't be able to see how dark it was, but you weren't having any of it. I've always found value in it; you can learn a lot about yourself in the hours you spend alone, in the dark."

Darrell smiled. "I don't remember that."

"Well, we remember what we need to."

When Darrell arrived back at his apartment, he didn't immediately go inside. He killed the ignition and sat there thinking while wind shook his car. He stole a glance at the scuffed face of his old Timex watch, given to him by a well-loved uncle who had been chased and outrun by cancer. Would Darrell's fate be similar? Withered and forlorn? The hours were gathering.

Was the camera watching him now? Had this already been filmed?

Stop it.

He could so easily go inside and view the tape; see what the time code was at the hour of his death. He could see where he was when it happened. A hospital bed? At home? Run down in the road somewhere?

Stop.

Exiting the car, Darrell began crossing the street, but something gave him pause, and he stopped midway. Cars passed on either side of him, horns blaring, his coat billowing in their wake. A skein of pigeons took flight from somewhere far behind him, their shadows wheeling across the blacktop, sliding over the fluid stream of roaring automobiles, up the sides of the row houses and across the sky, reduced to triangular shapes in a blur of motion, gathering in the wind. Flexing. Contracting. A muscle of many.

Stepping forward, Darrell passed between the rushing traffic, touched only by their trailing breath. Reaching the curb, he ascended the steps of his apartment, keyed the lock on the door, and pushed.

The next morning the garbage collector came early. The sun was shining, but the air was cold. The fall hadn't yet arrived, but it was coming.

.Acknowledgements

To my family, my friends, and to my English teachers, my humblest thanks for all the generous support and encouragement over the years, without which this fiction could not have been possible.

And to Beverley Daurio, who believed, my warmest gratitude.

.